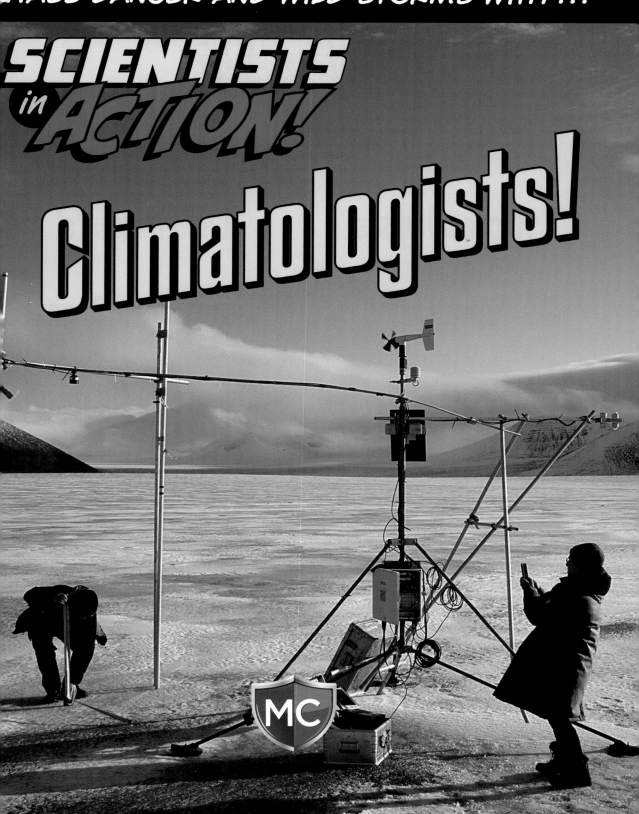

SCIENTISTS in ACTION!

Archaeologists!

Astronauts!

Big-Animal Vets!

Biomedical Engineers!

Civil Engineers!

Climatologists!

Crime Scene Techs!

Cyber Spy Hunters!

Marine Biologists!

Robot Builders!

Climatologists!

By Clifford Thompson

Mason Crest
450 Parkway Drive, Suite D
Broomall, PA 19008
www.masoncrest.com

Printed and bound in the United States of America.

Series ISBN: 978-1-4222-3416-7
Hardback ISBN: 978-1-4222-3422-8
EBook ISBN: 978-1-4222-8483-4

3 5 7 9 8 6 4 2

Produced by Shoreline Publishing Group LLC
Santa Barbara, California
Editorial Director: James Buckley Jr.
Designer: Tom Carling, Carling Design Inc.
Production: Sandy Gordon
www.shorelinepublishing.com

Cover image: Diane Burko

Library of Congress Cataloging-in-Publication Data
Thompson, Clifford, author.
    Climatologists! / by Clifford Thompson.
            pages cm. -- (Scientists in action!)
    Audience: Grades 9 to 12
Includes bibliographical references and index.
ISBN 978-1-4222-3422-8 (hardback : alk. paper) -- ISBN 978-1-4222-3416-7 (series : alk. paper) -- ISBN 978-1-
4222-8483-4 (ebook) 1. Climatology--Juvenile literature. 2. Climatologists--Juvenile literature. I. Title.
QC981.3.T54 2016
551.6--dc23
                                    2015004671

Contents

Key Icons to Look For

Words to Understand: These words with their easy-to-understand definitions will increase the reader's understanding of the text, while building vocabulary skills.

Sidebars: This boxed material within the main text allows readers to build knowledge, gain insights, explore possibilities, and broaden their perspectives by weaving together additional information to provide realistic and holistic perspectives.

Research Projects: Readers are pointed toward areas of further inquiry connected to each chapter. Suggestions are provided for projects that encourage deeper research and analysis.

Text-Dependent Questions: These questions send the reader back to the text for more careful attention to the evidence presented here.

Series Glossary of Key Terms: This back-of-the-book glossary contains terminology used throughout this series. Words found here increase the reader's ability to read and comprehend higher-level books and articles in this field.

Action!

The sky was gray, but that meant it was Rebecca Mazur's idea of a good day: cloudy with a chance of saving lives.

Days like that one are all part of her job as a **meteorologist** for the National Oceanic and Atmospheric Administration (NOAA). The agency hires climatologists and weather experts such as Rebecca who study and make predictions about weather, climate, and the atmosphere.

On that particular day, Mazur was driving in a part of southeast Wyoming where she knew severe storms could occur. She parked her car in a spot where she thought she had the best chance of seeing a big thunderstorm. Sure enough, a little northwest of her spot, over some nearby mountains, a storm began to develop.

WORDS TO UNDERSTAND

internships   jobs often done for free by people in the early stages of study for a career

meteorologist   a scientist who forecasts weather and weather patterns

Mazur looked at the laptop computer in her car. On the screen, with the help of radar images, she could see a storm making a loop as it moved east. She could also tell from the images what the weather in front of the storm was like. The storm was going to get much more intense.

Thanks to years of training, she was ready for it. Even when she was growing up in Illinois, the weather fascinated her. She always loved watching the skies, and she immersed herself in books and videos that explained the weather—or at least had really awesome pictures of it. Her main interest was thunderstorms, especially those that produce tornadoes. In sixth grade, she did a science project all about tornadoes, and she always went outside when she knew thunderstorms were coming, in case she could see a major twister.

Mazur carried that intense desire to know more about thunderstorms into adulthood. She became a SKYWARN weather spotter at the age of 18. To do that, she attended training sessions held by the National Weather Service. After a semester as a music major in college, she changed focus and pursued a degree in meteorology. Throughout her school years, she got **internships** in both research and forecasting, wanting to know everything she could about how the atmosphere works. During that time, she also learned how to storm chase.

Now, sitting in her car and waiting for the storm, she felt excited about what she would see. She had a direct view of where the storm would unfold. Within half an hour, the storm moved away from the mountains and into the moist air. The storm itself was tall like a mountain, looming overhead, and it began to show signs of rotating. The base of the storm was very dark and shaped like a horseshoe with the ends pointed away from her. To the right of the "horseshoe," Mazur could see a shaft of rain and hail—what looked like a solid gray-white wall with a hint of turquoise. From those colors, Mazur judged that the hail was large, so she needed to be careful, or her car would get some big dents—to say nothing of what the hard stones could do to her.

An oncoming storm is a happy occasion for weather expert Rebecca Mazur. She has made it her life's work to find and track these storms. By understanding and predicting them, she can help save lives.

The rotating winds of the storm system gathered speed and eventually formed the familiar cone of a tornado. Some tornadoes can reach wind speeds of more than 200 miles per hour (322 kph).

Where the base of the horseshoe met the wall of rain and hail, the clouds came down and began a wild dance, moving in different directions, including up into the main storm tower. If there was going to be a tornado, this area—the wall cloud—was where it would occur.

With her camera ready, Mazur carefully watched the storm organize. Sometimes, rotating storms produce tornadoes, and she wanted to capture every second of the event. She had her phone ready, too: as a meteorologist, she had a duty to report her observations to the local

National Weather Service office, especially if there was a good chance that a storm would produce a tornado. Real-time reports from the field are crucial in alerting people who are in the path of dangerous weather.

Soon, Mazur watched as a funnel cloud developed. A tornado! Quickly, she reported her sighting to the National Weather Service, knowing that they would issue weather warnings. With her report, they were able to inform the public that the tornado threat from this storm was very high. The storm ended up producing a tornado for roughly 20 minutes, and Mazur was able to witness and report on its entire life.

Mazur had a great feeling, knowing that her forecast panned out perfectly, and that she was able to provide detailed and timely reports of the tornado. After it was over, she was able to talk to some of the people living in that area who were affected by the tornado. Many had heard the warnings in time to seek shelter. Rebecca had provided information to help people make good decisions in a critical time.

She was also happy that she had been able to take what she learned in school out to the real world, to compare theory from her books with the live atmosphere. With work that combined research and weather forecasting, she had found her dream job.

The Scientists and Their Science

Your history teacher tells you what people did decades, or even centuries, before any of us were born. Sometimes, understanding history gives us an idea of what can happen in years to come because events such as wars and economic depressions often repeat themselves. So a person who understands history can sometimes make predictions about the future.

A climatologist is like a history teacher. The difference is that a climatologist studies past patterns and changes in climates, to help predict

WORDS TO UNDERSTAND

atmospheric science   the study of the atmosphere, the gases that surround the Earth

glaciers   huge sheets of ice covering a landmass

inquisitiveness   being curious, asking questions to learn more

traits   particular qualities belonging to a person

Weather vs. Climate

There is a difference between weather and climate. Weather describes what is happening in the atmosphere in a short period of time. Climate describes long-term weather patterns, or the type of environment of a particular area or place. When scientists talk about changes in the weather, they're talking about hours or perhaps days. When they discuss climate, they're looking at weather patterns over years, decades, or even longer time periods.

changes that will occur months or years in the future. That information is very important for all kinds of reasons. For example, predicting how much rain a particular area will receive helps farmers make plans for growing crops. That has an effect on the food we all eat.

A meteorologist is more like a TV news reporter than a history teacher. (In fact, some meteorologists are on TV news shows.) Unlike a history teacher, who tells us what happened long ago, a reporter tells us what is happening right now or what will happen in the next few days. A meteorologist does that, too—for the weather. Have you ever watched the TV news or looked on the Internet to find out if you should take an umbrella when you leave home? That information is given to you by meteorologists.

Climatologists and meteorologists have a lot in common, though. For one thing, both perform research. Unlike a TV meteorologist, research meteorologists collect and study data on the weather. Sometimes that means getting very close to the action when there is a tornado or hurricane to understand how they work. Climatologists do research, too, studying past conditions and using computer programs to understand how weather operates over long periods. With computers, climatologists and meteorologists create weather models to predict how weather will

Most people are familiar with this kind of meterologist: the television professional who is also a trained scientist. By providing information about the weather, these experts help people plan their lives.

operate. In both cases, that often means heading into the field to find information, whether that field is in the icy Arctic or a burning desert. Scientists like these have to go where the action is!

To become a climatologist, you usually need a master's degree in **atmospheric science**, and sometimes a Ph.D. is required. Some who go on to become climatologists study math, engineering, or physics as undergraduates. In addition to a background in math and science, climatology requires an understanding of computers and computer programming. Meteorologists who appear on TV sometimes have just bachelor's degrees, but to work as a meteorologist for a government agency, you often need a master's degree or Ph.D.

Climate Change

In studying climate history, climatologists have reached different conclusions about the causes of recent changes in weather. Many climatologists believe that human activity, like the use of gasoline to power cars, has added dangerous amounts of carbon to Earth's atmosphere. Those scientists believe that higher carbon levels are the reason we have seen hotter summers, melting **glaciers**,

The amount of carbon put out by human activity—including from cars or from smokestacks such as these—helped make 2014 the warmest year ever recorded.

One dangerous effect of climate change is the rapid warming of northern regions, home to glaciers such as this one, which are melting at a much faster pace than in past years.

rising sea levels, and unusual numbers of tornadoes and hurricanes. Climatologists have said that we must take steps to stop polluting the atmosphere before it's too late, and they warn that time is running out to avoid disaster.

For years, people used the term "global warming" when talking about the effect of pollution on the planet. These days, the term "climate change" is more common, because the changes are thought to go beyond rising temperatures. The effects of climate change would include droughts that affect food supplies, cities and other areas permanently under water, frequent severe weather such as tornadoes, and widespread harm to wildlife.

More and more people around the world are calling for governments to take major steps to control the production of greenhouse gases that contribute to climate change.

Some other climatologists, though, feel that Earth has certain weather patterns of its own that are not connected to human activity. According to them, the natural course of the atmosphere is to get cooler or warmer during certain periods. Climate change and its causes are the subjects of heated debate all over the world.

What It Takes

What personal **traits** are useful if you want to be a climatologist or meteorologist? "For research, the most important trait is curiosity," says John Nielsen-Gammon, the Texas state climatologist and a professor at Texas A&M University. "You have to wonder about how things work and relate to each other in order to expand what we know.

"Since I do a lot of talking with the public and the press as part of my role as state climatologist, I also need a thick skin. Whenever I say something specific about climate change, I know that many people will be infuriated, just because climate change is so political and people keep hearing that the other side [whichever side that happens to be] is corrupt or closed-minded. I could take the easy way out and not talk about climate change at all, but then I'd be denying the public the benefit of everything I've learned."

Nielsen-Gammon studied at MIT (the Massachusetts Institute of

Nielsen-Gammon works in his office at Texas A&M University. He uses his position as the Texas state climatologist to help spread the word about the problems caused by climate change.

Technology). "When I became Texas state climatologist, I wasn't really a climatologist," he says. "I'd never done any research in that area, and I'd only taken one or two classes on the subject at MIT. I knew about weather data, though, and climate observations are simply observations of the weather over a long time. I started focusing on the climate of Texas, then on climate change, and eventually became a mostly self-taught expert."

Another important trait is "perseverance," says the meteorologist Howard Bluestein, who teaches at the University

Weather stations such as this one provides important information for climatologists.

of Oklahoma. That is because "so many things can go wrong when [you're] trying to collect...radar data in a tornado, that one must keep trying again and again and again." Like Nielsen-Gammon, Bluestein studied at MIT. He also says that it is important to have **inquisitiveness**, a drive to find out why things happen, because it provides the motivation to try to do something difficult and dangerous like collecting mobile radar data near tornadoes and then analyzing and interpreting the data." A meteorologist also needs the "ability to stay calm under pressure, because many decisions have to be made perfectly, very quickly, in order to stay safe and successfully collect data," Bluestein says.

"Skills that I find essential to my career," Rebecca Mazur says, "include having good critical thinking and reasoning skills, being a good communicator, and generally being able to work well with others. There is a lot of data to sort through when making weather forecasts, and sometimes finding the answer can be very hard when different weather models tell you that different things are going to happen."

About being a meteorologist, Mazur says: "You can make the best forecast in the world, but if you do not relay the information in an easy-to-understand manner that will help folks make good decisions on how to protect themselves and their families, unfortunate things can happen. Oftentimes, the weather forecasting business is a team effort, so being able to work well with others is a good skill to have in your back pocket."

 # Text-Dependent Questions

1. Name two traits a climatologist should have.
2. For what state is John Nielsen-Gammon the state climatologist?
3. Name three possible negative effects of climate change.

 # Research Project

Contact a meteorologist who works at a TV or radio station near you, or read about them online. Find out where they went to school and what degrees they earned, as well as why they became interested in their work.

Tools of the Trade

*T*he most important "tool" for any scientist is his or her brain. With years of study, knowledge of scientific principles, and built-in curiosity, scientists put that tool to work every day. To provide the data they need for their studies, however, they also rely on a wide range of techniques, tools, and technology. Climatologists need much more information than they can get from simply going outside and feeling the temperature. Gathering data to interpret takes a lot of effort, some travel, patience . . . and some cool gear. Read on to find out how trucks, balloons, and even World War II technology are part of the climatologists' toolbox.

WORDS TO UNDERSTAND

geostationary   remaining in the same place above the Earth during an orbit

radiosonde   a device sent aloft to measure atmospheric conditions

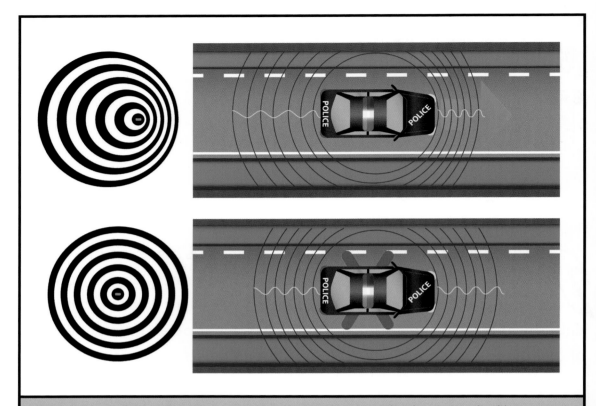

The police car in the top diagram is moving, so the sound moves with it, but in a predictable pattern: the Doppler effect. With a steady pattern, the car in the bottom shows how a stationary car compares.

The Doppler Effect

*T*he Austrian physicist Johann Christian Doppler (1803–1853) didn't do much that was connected with climate or weather, except for one thing. In 1842, Doppler explained something important that had to do with sound and movement. What he explained became important for predicting weather.

Have you ever noticed that a moving vehicle that makes noise, such as an ambulance, makes a lower sound when it's far away from you, a higher sound when it's near you, and a lower sound again when it has passed you? That happens because sound travels in waves, and the farther the sound is from you, the longer the sound waves take to reach you. The longer the sound waves take to reach you, the lower the frequency of the waves—and the lower the frequency, the lower the sound in your ears. When the ambulance is right beside you, the waves reach you right away, the frequency of the waves increases, and the sound is higher. As the ambulance moves away again, the frequency of the waves lowers again, and so does the tone. This is called the Doppler effect.

When it comes to making predictions about weather, this Doppler effect combines with something else: the way echoes work. Sound waves bounce off surfaces, and the sound comes back to you in what is called an echo. The closer the surface is to you, the sooner you hear

The next time you hear a siren coming toward you, notice how the pattern of the sound changes as the vehicle first approaches you, reaches you, and then races past. That's Doppler in action.

the echo. If you say "hello" and get a quick "hello" back, even though no one else is there, the sound waves from your voice have bounced off a surface close by.

Instead of sound waves, meteorologists use Doppler radar to send out silent radio waves. When the waves bounce back from an object, meteorologists look at their frequency (or the Doppler effect) to tell where the object is and how quickly it is moving. In this way, scientists can spot storms and tell how fast their winds are moving. That is how meteorologists can predict hurricanes and tornadoes.

Weather Balloons

Every day, scientists send up weather balloons. About five feet (1.5 m) wide and filled with helium, the balloon rises through the atmosphere with a **radiosonde** attached. The radiosonde is a

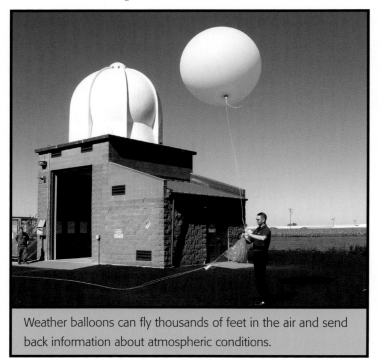

Weather balloons can fly thousands of feet in the air and send back information about atmospheric conditions.

lightweight box, made of cardboard, that contains instruments for measuring conditions in the atmosphere. As the balloon rises, it expands, until it is the size of a car or bigger. Just before it reaches outer space, the balloon bursts, the radiosonde falls back toward Earth, and a parachute inflates to slow its fall. It lands miles from where it was sent up. By downloading the information from the radiosonde, scientists can learn about the conditions high above and then study how that affects weather and climate on Earth.

Computers

Climatologists use computers to study data about the weather and see how it changes over time.

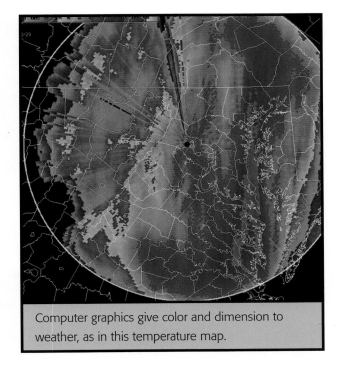

Computer graphics give color and dimension to weather, as in this temperature map.

Computers are also useful for predicting what the weather will do. This works in a couple of different ways. For example, looking at computer records for what the temperature has been on the same date in a particular place over the years, scientists have an idea of what the weather will be on that date this year. Also, scientists can look at present conditions in the atmosphere, then use computer data to see what the weather was like at other times under the same conditions. That way, they have an idea of what the weather will be.

Instrument Pods

Storm chasers, or those who study and follow the paths of tornadoes and hurricanes, sometimes use instrument pods. These sets of small instruments are placed on the ground near storms. They take pictures of what happens inside storms, and they measure

With the vast amount of weather data pouring in from so many sources, computers play a big part in helping climatologists interpret the information and share their findings.

temperature, humidity, and wind speed. The dangerous thing about putting instrument pods in place is that you have to get pretty close to the storm yourself. To avoid harm while placing the instruments correctly, scientists have to remember what they learned from years of study, and at the same time keep their wits about them. A handful of storm chasers have been killed or injured when the storms moved too fast for them to escape. This is not a job for the fainthearted!

Trucks

Because of the danger of chasing storms, not everyone wants to do it—but a lot of people like to watch it. With that in mind, Discovery Channel aired a show called *Storm Chasers* for several seasons beginning in 2007. Sean Casey, who directed the series, designed a special vehicle for following tornadoes and hurricanes. The first Tornado Intercept Vehicle, or TIV 1, was built in the early 2000s. It was a heavily armored vehicle with metal parts close to the ground to keep it from being tossed around by strong winds. The problem was that all the armor weighed so much that the vehicle could barely keep up with the storms, and the low-hanging metal parts collided with all kinds of debris. To solve those problems, Casey designed the TIV 2. The TIVs are outfitted with meteorological equipment to get data on the storms. Next up, Casey says to look for TIV 3.

Floating for Science

As people debate what causes climate change, a missing piece of the puzzle is how the oceans interact with the atmosphere. The transfer of heat between sea and sky is called "heat flux." The movement of heat from the ocean to the sky helps cause winter storms and hurricanes. To help understand how this works, climatologists at the Space Science Engineering Center at the University of Wisconsin at Madison are testing devices the size of Frisbees that can ride ocean currents atop waves and send data to satellites.

Satellites

A satellite is something that goes around, or orbits, something else. A weather satellite is a piece of equipment that orbits Earth. There are two kinds of weather satellites.

Satellites in **geostationary** orbit fly very high, more than 21,000 miles (35,000 km) above the ground. They seem to be unmoving because they move at the same pace that the planet rotates. In that way, they take photos of the same region of the Earth, recording weather activity there, and they transmit the photos to the ground. A series of photographs shows cloud movement and allows scientists to predict the paths of storms.

Using cameras and sensors aimed at parts of the Earth, satellites give a bird's-eye view of the weather. They continuously monitor weather patterns so that scientists can make their predictions.

Satellites in polar orbit move north to south as the planet rotates eastward. Every time the satellite makes a complete pass around the globe, it records a different narrow area. Together, those narrow slices produce a picture of a large area. These satellites are only about 525 miles (850 km) above Earth, so they produce more detailed pictures of cloud systems and storms.

 # Text-Dependent Questions

1. How does the Doppler effect help predict weather?
2. How do climatologists use instrument pods?
3. What do you call people who seek out bad weather to record it?

 # Research Project

Have you ever been in a terrible storm? Research thunderstorms, hailstorms, tornadoes, or hurricanes in your area. What are the five worst weather events ever in your city or state?

Tales From the Field!

Every scientist has to spend at least some time indoors, in labs or libraries. Studying the weather and the climate, though, means that these scientists can't spend all their time indoors. They have to get out into the world . . . where the weather is. Climatology can also take them many places, some of them exciting . . . and even dangerous.

WORDS TO UNDERSTAND

carbon dioxide the gas that humans breathe out, as well as a gas that is part of the exhaust from engines and factories

deployed placed, arranged, or set up equipment or manpower

humidity the amount of moisture in the air

innocuous seemingly harmless

latitudes imaginary bands around the Earth that divide the globe into measurable chunks

supercell a massive gathering of smaller storms that combine to form a single, large storm system

Luck and Mysteries

Sometimes, in addition to training, preparation, curiosity, bravery, and perseverance, a weather scientist needs a little luck. One day in May of 2007, Howard Bluestein's team appeared at first to be out of luck. They were in rural Kansas, looking for a tornado, when two things went wrong at once. As they rode in a truck with radar equipment attached, one of their tires blew out. Meanwhile, they discovered that a tornado-like storm was gathering in western Oklahoma, miles from where they had been on the lookout—at a moment when their truck was out of commission.

The team had their truck towed to a nearby town, where it took hours to find a replacement tire. Then their luck improved: In the area they had planned to watch, storms approached from Oklahoma. "We **deployed** the radar just east of Protection, Kansas," Bluestein recalls, "and while we were scanning, what had been an **innocuous** storm developed into a **supercell** that produced a number of tornadoes."

A supercell forms when moist air close to the ground warms and begins to rise. Soon it reaches hot, dryer air between a half-mile to one mile (1–2 km) above ground. Flat-topped clouds are created, sometimes pen-

The anemometer on the upper right tells wind speed. The arrow at the back shows wind direction.

Tornadoes are among the most destructive storms in the world, with winds that can fling cars around and pull houses apart. The United States is hit by more tornadoes than any other country.

etrating cooler air above them. That, in turn, creates an updraft. If it rotates, with the help of winds in the area, it can form a mesocyclone, which forms a tornado. (One in five supercells creates a tornado.)

That is what happened on that day in May of 2007. Not everyone was lucky that day: The largest tornado devastated the town of Greensburg, Kansas. In aiming the radar at the tornadoes and studying their data, Bluestein and the others made a discovery: "We found that the eye of the tornado extended from near the surface all the way up to the top of the storm," Bluestein says. The eye of a tornado is the almost circular, relatively calm area in the middle. Learning about the eye of a tornado can help scientists understand how the tornadoes themselves work. Still, a mystery remains about the eye's extending from near the surface to the top. "We still don't really understand completely why," Bluestein says. Scientists must face the fact that they still don't know all the answers.

VORTEX2

*I*n May of 2009, more than 100 researchers, armed with a vast array of equipment, set out to document the life of a tornado, from start to finish. The project would take two years and cost about $12 million. It was known as Verification of the Origin of Rotation in Tornadoes Experiment, or VORTEX2. A similar project, called VORTEX1, had been carried out in the mid-1990s. Meteorologist Joshua Wurman, who is now president of the Center for Severe Weather Research in Boulder, Colo., was involved in both projects. The VORTEX2 team covered "Tornado Alley," the long stretch between the Appalachian Mountains and the Rocky Mountains, waiting for twisters.

At about four o'clock in the afternoon on June 5, outside the town of La Grange, Wyoming, the team got what it wanted. A lot of clouds began swirling, and one of them, long and thin, touched the ground—a tornado. It was time to go into action.

With the tornado coming toward them, the team began setting up a dozen instrument pods on the ground, about 500 feet (150 m) apart. Each pod had sensors to measure the temperature, **humidity**, and wind speed, and each had a pair of cameras. The team had to rush to set up the pods, then move away again quickly before the tornado got too close. They barely made it. By the time they finished deploying the equipment and were back in their vehicles, the gray tornado was about a quarter-mile behind them, spinning across a road, making a deafening racket, and causing the vehicles to rock back and forth.

The team escaped. Later, the team members were later able to study the data, and they made some discoveries. The instruments' Doppler radar took a picture of a supercell once per minute and produced 30 detailed images. From those, Wurman and the others figured out that a strong, downward-moving air current at the back of the tornado may be responsible for creating it. The current is called the rear flank downdraft, or RFD. "Without this downdraft," Wurman told reporter Will Gray for the publication *New Scientist*, "it's very difficult to spin up a tornado."

Very Cold Places

Dr. Paul Mayewski is director of the Climate Change Institute at the University of Maine. He warns that "the rise in CO_2 [**carbon dioxide** in the atmosphere] is 100 times faster than anything in the last million years," as Olivia Kefauver reported for the Colby College publication, *The Colby Echo*. Mayewski has led teams of researchers to some of the coldest places on Earth to study ice cores. An ice core is a long, thin tube cut deep into a layer of ice. By studying the ice at different depths or looking at the objects he has found in the ice

Thick polar ice holds a lot of information, and core-sample drilling can reveal it.

cores, Mayewski has learned a lot about the effects of environmental conditions on the planet. His travels have taken him to Antarctica, Greenland, and the Himalayas, where his team was the first to get ice cores.

Mayewski discovered from the ice cores that instead of being extremely slow, as many had thought, significant climate changes can happen in just a few years. "What's happening today already is dramatic," he said, according to Kefauver. However, he also believes that we can fight climate change. "We can easily have a much better quality of life," he said. "There is a very bright future for people who are innovative and creative."

Sometimes, It's the Weather

Several years ago, John Nielsen-Gammon was in charge of making forecasts about the weather and pollution in Houston. Research aircraft, equipped with devices for measuring different types of air pollution, were going to be sent out to polluted areas. It was Nielsen-Gammon's job to say where they should be sent—and he needed to be right because the cost of flying a research aircraft was $100,000 for one hour!

Early in the first week of research, Nielsen-Gammon realized that the winds in Houston were not doing what he expected. "Instead of

Nielsen-Gammon's research showed a new way to deal with the smog that often blanketed the southern Texas city of Houston.

the wind blowing from water to land during the day and from land to water at night, like normal sea and land breezes, it was doing almost the opposite," he explains. That was important to know because winds had a lot to do with where pollution occurred.

Doing more research, Nielsen-Gammon discovered that 20 years earlier, other scientists had come up with a theory about sea breezes at different **latitudes**. The theory involved a mathematical formula. According to this theory, at one particular latitude, a sea breeze would be very strong and last a long time, and it would not blow at its normal time. That latitude was 30 degrees, which turned out to be the latitude of Houston! Nielsen-Gammon had found the first solid evidence to back up a two-decade-old theory.

Now that he knew what the wind ought to be doing, Nielsen-Gammon could predict the motion of air pollution much more accurately. He also figured out that the large-scale winds and the sea breeze interact in a very special way to produce several hours of stagnant, highly polluted air in a very small portion of the city. Before he made his discovery, everybody had thought that one or two human-made sources were to blame when a small portion of the city became polluted. "I showed that, at least sometimes, it's not the polluters, it's the weather," Nielsen-Gammon says.

Helping the Country

Climatologists can easily make an impact on their local area, but in some cases, they can help spur change on a larger scale.

"In 2011, the Texas drought had just shattered all statewide records for hottest summer and driest twelve months on record," says Nielsen-Gammon. "The state was receiving a lot of national attention because of the drought. At the same time, our governor, Rick Perry, was running for the Republican nomination for president, and many people were critical of his position on climate change." (Governor Perry didn't believe that climate change was caused by man.)

"I took it upon myself to analyze the history of drought in Texas and to write a series of blog posts discussing the extent to which the drought was caused or enhanced by climate change," Nielsen-Gammon says. "My blog drew national attention, and it seems that many people liked the way that I told the story of the drought and its context without shading my description to fit one political point of view or another.

What to do about climate change is often debated in Congressional hearing rooms such as this one. Governments around the world are looking for laws and ways of living that can slow climate change.

"In late October, I was formally invited to help give a congressional briefing on Capitol Hill [in Washington, D.C.] on the relationship between extreme weather events and climate change. It felt good to learn that the research I had done was considered valuable enough to be worth telling to members of Congress and their staff. I was also pleased that they thought I could communicate the information effectively.

"Inside, I was afraid that I would be exposed as a know-nothing idiot, especially since I would be sharing the podium with an international business executive and a world-famous scientist. They set us up in a room in one of the House Office Buildings. I didn't seem to make any mistakes in my talk, and I fielded and accurately answered my share of questions. So I helped my country and didn't make a fool of myself!"

Mother Nature Has the Last Word

"In one particular instance," weather scientist Rebecca Mazur says, "I was a part of a forecast team dealing with the possibility of a major winter storm in our area. In the days leading up to the event, the weather models were foretelling blizzard conditions for most of the event, which is a major danger to persons traveling through our area and could be deadly for livestock.

"The combination of strong winds and heavy snow were expected for a good part of the day, and so we added strong wording to our forecast statements so that people knew this was not a storm to take lightly. Unfortunately, the storm moved about one hundred miles further south than we thought it would go, and the heavy snow never materialized. Our customers were not too happy with us, and I was extremely frustrated since I hate disappointing the people I serve, especially when all the data was pointing toward a major winter event.

"This event taught me a big lesson in humility, and that no matter how much I think I have Mother Nature figured out, she always has the last word. Also, I learned the importance of looking back into the history books and comparing current data to previous events, because computer models do not have all the answers, and experience plays a big role in the science of forecasting.

"This event also helped me reevaluate the way I communicate weather information, especially in advance of potentially dangerous conditions, so that the public can make the appropriate decisions on how to prepare for the weather."

 # Text-Dependent Questions

1. What gas is a clue to the effects of climate change?

2. What is one of the names of a storm that will produce a tornado?

3. In what city did the Texas state climatologist make his discoveries about wind-aided pollution?

 # Research Project

Climate change: What is the science? As we've seen, there is a bit of debate. Read the information you can find on reputable sites, such as universities, governments, or science institutes. Compare them and see what you think of the discussion.

Scientists in the News

Prize Winner: Ann Henderson-Sellers is one of today's most important figures in studying climate change and predicting climate patterns. She was a member of the Intergovernmental Panel on Climate Change, which won the Nobel Peace Prize in 2007 for helping to spread knowledge about human-made climate change and for helping point to solutions.

Henderson-Sellers was born in 1952 in England. Interested in science from childhood, she studied mathematics at Bristol University. She became particularly fascinated by the atmospheres of planets and earned a doctorate in atmospheric science in 1976 from Leicester University. Her thesis focused on the greenhouse effect, or the warming of Earth's atmosphere from the burning of fossil fuels.

In her position as tropical climatologist at Liverpool University, Henderson-Sellers learned even more about how the environment affects people, and vice versa. She has been very vocal about the need to reverse climate change. She has written more than a dozen books and more than 500 papers.

Speaking Out: Climatologist James E. Hansen was born in 1941 and grew up in a small town in Iowa. He worked for 46 years for the

National Aeronautics and Space Administration (NASA) at the Goddard Institute for Space Studies, in New York City.

James E. Hansen

Hansen started out by studying the planet Venus. Then, in the 1970s, he began to focus more on Earth, writing about the bad effects of human-made greenhouse gases. He argued that those effects would build on one another to change the climate and make sea levels rise, which would cause flooding around the world.

Hansen has said many times that we need to get busy reversing climate change. In 1988, he testified before Congress; the hottest years on record have all occurred since his testimony. In 2005, when an official in George W. Bush's White House began trying to control what Hansen was saying, Hansen became even more vocal instead of backing down. Since then, he has left government service and become an activist for fighting climate change.

Hurricane Expert: Steve Lyons, a famous meteorologist, worked for The Weather Channel for 12 seasons before being named in 2010 as head meteorologist at the National Weather Service's forecast office in San Angelo, Texas. Lyons was born in 1954 and grew up in southern California. He worked for the National Hurricane Center before joining The Weather Channel in 1998. Lyons became known as an expert in severe weather, giving clear explanations of what was happening as hurricanes and tropical storms approached. He has also written many articles and reports. Asked why he wanted to move to Texas, he said that it is his favorite state because he loves "the wild weather" there.

Find Out More

Books

Hollingshead, Mike and Nguyen, Eric. *Adventures in Tornado Alley: The Storm Chasers*. New York: Thames & Hudson, 2008.

Logan, LaVerne and Powers, Don. *Meteorology: Atmosphere and Weather (Expanding Science Skills Series)*. Quincy, Ill.: Mark Twain Media, 2010.

Miller, Ron. *Chasing the Storm: Tornadoes, Meteorology, and Weather Watching*. Minneapolis: Twenty-First Century Books, 2013.

Woodward, John. *Climate Change (DK Eyewitness Books)*. New York: DK Publishing, 2008.

Web Sites

www.ametsoc.org
The official site of the American Meteorological Society, it offers lots of information for students who wish to study meteorology, and about careers in the field.

www.epa.gov/climatechange/
The Web site of the United States Environmental Protection Agency includes details about climate change and what we can do about it.

Series Glossary of Key Terms

airlock   a room on a space station from which astronauts can move from inside to outside the station and back

anatomy   a branch of knowledge that deals with the structure of organisms

bionic   to be assisted by mechanical movements

carbon dioxide   a gas that is in the air that we breathe out

classified   kept secret from all but a few people in a government or an organization

deforestation   the destruction of forest or woodland

diagnose   to recognize by signs and symptoms

discipline   in science, this means a particular field of study

elite   the part or group having the highest quality or importance

genes   information stored in cells that determine a person's physical characteristics

geostationary   remaining in the same place above the Earth during an orbit

innovative   groundbreaking, original

inquisitiveness   an ability to be curious, to continue asking questions to learn more

internships   jobs often done for free by people in the early stages of study for a career

marine   having to do with the ocean

meteorologist   a scientist who forecasts weather and weather patterns

physicist   a scientist who studies physics, which examines how matter and energy move and relate

primate   a type of four-limbed mammal with a developed brain; includes humans, apes, and monkeys

traits   a particular quality or personality belonging to a person

Index

Photo Credits

About the Author

Clifford Thompson is the former editor in chief of *Current Biography*, a monthly magazine and annual book. In 2014, he received a Whiting Writers' Award for nonfiction for his book *Love for Sale and Other Essays*. He lives in Brooklyn, N.Y.